CHARMED

(GUARDIAN ACADEMY, #6)

JESSICA SORENSEN

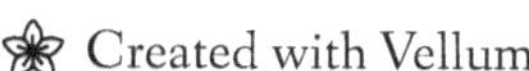
Created with Vellum

ALANÁ

"Oh my God," I groan, trying not to lose my mind. But I feel like banging my head against the window. Jax is driving me absolutely crazy. "You're crazy. You really are."

He throws me a dirty look as he steers down the highway. "*I'm* the crazy one?" He picks up a bottle of soda. "You're the one who thinks a vampire is stronger than a werewolf."

"I never said stronger," I correct. "I just said deadlier, but not necessarily to a werewolf. Just other creatures in general."

He twists the cap off the bottle of soda. "Werewolves are way deadlier than vampires. Trust me."

"No way. Vampires have fangs, blood lust, mind compulsion, super speed, crazy hearing." I jot off a list.

"Werewolves are strong, have less weaknesses, can bond someone to them." He briefly pauses, an edgy look flashing across his face.

He's done that a lot over the last handful of hours, ever

since we fled the academy, and set out on our own. We haven't told anyone why we left or even that we took off. We simply snuck into the school, packed as much stuff as we could, hopped in Jax's car, and sped off.

Our plan is to stay clear of the school, and anyone connected to it, until we can figure out what in the crazy faeries is going on with... Well, a lot of things. Finding out who the real leader of the Electi is, which so far, we know is a shapeshifter who took my grandfather's identity. We also need to figure out what Vivianne is up to, if she for sure is the fey princess and why I saw her hanging out in the woods in the middle of the night with the queen of the water fey. Another problem we're trying to solve is if Dash is alive. I left a message on Thad's voicemail to see what he knows about that, but he hasn't called me back yet. And then there's the problem of figuring out what kind of creature I am, and that has become our top priority at the moment. We sent Ollie out to find the answer, but we haven't heard from him since we parted ways. It has both of us very worried, since he was searching for the Scrawl of Secrets in Hushing Forest, a place that only pixies know the location to.

"I don't know about the bonding part," I tell Jax and then pop a couple of chips into my mouth. "Seeing as how you weren't able to bond to me."

He takes a sip of the soda. "That's only because you're an anomaly."

Which basically means I'm a freak, but Jax is refusing to say that. I don't know why. The Jax I first met totally would've. But ever since the whole biting incident, he's been acting like a straight-up weirdo. My bet is spending hours possessed messed with his mind. I just hope he returns to his normal self soon, because this nice guy vibe he's giving off is making me feel off balance.

"You say anomaly. I say freak." I quip, slipping off my sandals and putting my feet onto the dashboard.

It's late in the evening, but warm. Since the air-conditioning doesn't work well, I have my window down, and the cool autumn breeze is gusting into the cab and blowing strands of my long brown hair into my violet eyes.

"You should stop calling yourself that." He slips on a pair of sunglasses, covering up his silver eyes. His light brown hair is a mess due to the wind blowing through it for the last several hours, and yet somehow, it looks intentionally styled that way.

"What? Freak?" I give him a funny look. "Why? It doesn't bother me."

"Yeah, but..." He stares ahead at the road we're cruising down that's located in the middle of nowhere; only trees, fields, and shallow hills are nearby. I'm not even sure where we are. And I haven't seen anything but trees and land for hours. "Just because you're different, doesn't mean you're a freak. And it's not like we even know what you are."

"Yeah, so what? Being an unknown, different, rare creature kind of makes me a freak." I tuck a strand of my hair behind my ear. "But like I said, I'm totally cool with that."

"Oh, Alana." He quietly sighs underneath his breath.

"Oh, Jax." I mimic his sigh, then narrow my eyes at him. "Why are you acting like this?"

"Like what?" He feigns dumb, but I detect a slight twitch in his jaw.

I observe him, trying to see through this weird nice guy

act he's putting on. "You're being nice to me. Well, at least nice for you, and it's weird. You've never been nice to me."

"I've never been nice to you?" he questions, his brow meticulously arching. "Seriously?"

"Yes, seriously," I say. When he continues to stare at me unconvinced, I add. "Okay, I guess there's been a couple of times where you've been decent to me, but those moments are rare." I dazzle him with a cheeky smile. "Not that I care. I kind of prefer the moody Jax over this weird, nice one."

He rolls his eyes. "Only you'd prefer me to be an asshole."

"I don't want you to be an asshole," I clarify. "I just..." *You just what, Alana? Miss bantering with him? Miss him making you feel challenged?*

Miss him?

For the love of all magic, what is wrong with me?

"You just what?" he taunts with a challenge in his eyes.

I hate how my mind and body react to that challenge, hate that spark I feel buzzing underneath my skin.

"Nothing." I change the subject. "How much longer until we get there?" And by there, I mean to a place Jax insists pixies navigate to.

Although he didn't give me any specifics as to what this place is, it's location, or how he's even aware that it exists.

"Probably another fifteen minutes or so," he replies, his gaze burrowing into me.

The longer he stares at me, the more I want to squirm. But I tell my body to hold the freakin' faeries still, that we are so not going there with Jax, the brooding version or the nice one.

"You know, it's unsafe not to look at the road while

you're driving." I glance at him. "And if you crash, not everyone in this car has super healing powers."

He searches my eyes, for what, who the crazy trolls knows. "Maybe you do."

"Have super healing powers?" I snort a laugh. "I know I don't. Trust me; I've got scars all over my body to prove that."

"Maybe your powers were just delayed, and now they're finally manifesting. Delayed powers sometimes happen in certain creatures. Like for instance, certain types of fey. Some of them don't have any powers until they reach puberty."

"I'm well past puberty, though," I point out while grabbing another handful of chips. "But maybe you're right. Maybe my powers were delayed until I got my guardian mark since both of them coincided with each other. Well, that and my grandpa's death, but..." I bite down on my lip as images of seeing my grandpa dead flood my thoughts. "But anyway," I clear my throat, "All of that stuff happened around the same time."

Jax's brows knit as he looks at the road. At first, I think he's trying to figure out where we are, but then his gaze welds with mine.

"It's kind of strange all of that happened at the same time," he says. "And you got your guardian mark later than most guardians."

"What're you getting at? Because it seems like you're getting at something."

"I'm not necessarily getting at anything." He shifts to a lower gear, slowing down the car. "I'm just wondering something."

"What?" I lower my feet from the dash and glance

around at the fields, searching for a reason as to why he's slowing down.

All I can see is a narrow, bumpy dirt road that winds into the trees. Is that where we're going? Into the woods? Because the last time we wandered into the woods, he bit me.

The car comes to almost a complete stop as he turns onto the dirt road.

So yep, we're going into the woods. And nothing good has ever happened in the freakin' woods.

"Well, I don't know for certain," he says as he steers down the dirt road. "But I'm wondering if maybe someone was making your powers dormant."

My eyes widen. "You think someone was intentionally hiding my powers?"

His gaze sweeps across the trees and the branches canopying the road.

"I'm not sure," he mumbles. "It's just a thought I had."

My mind is spinning over the idea. "Who would do that, though? My parents?"

No, there's no way they'd keep something like that from me.

He shrugs, wariness creeping across his expression. "Honestly, and I could be wrong about all of this, but my best guess is that if someone was keeping your powers hidden, it was probably your grandfather."

I want to protest. Want to say there's no way that could be true. But over the last month or two, I've learned that my grandpa wasn't necessarily the man I thought he was, that he lived a secret life.

I sink back into the seat. "Why would he do that, though? What's the point of keeping my powers hidden?"

"Maybe to protect you from the ..." He lowers his voice. "Electi." He gives a short pause before quickly adding, "But again, I'm not sure. This is all just a guess. However, your grandpa worked hard to keep a lot of things hidden, and I'm wondering if somehow he knew about your powers, and maybe he knew the leader of the Electi would want you because of them, so he found a way to keep them dormant. But then he died and..." He offers me an apologetic look.

Agony sears inside me, but I stifle the feeling, focusing on what Jax said, unsure how I feel about his theory. There could be a ton of reasons why my powers have remained dormant until recently. But it is kind of coincidental that they made a grand appearance shortly after my grandpa died.

"Do you think my grandpa did some sort of connection spell to keep my powers hidden?" I ask, but it's not really a question. I'm just thinking aloud. "And then when he died, that connection broke?" I can't help thinking about all the times I've heard my grandpa's voice inside my head, giving me vague warnings about the future.

I had believed he was doing it because he is—was a foreseer—and saw an impending doom waiting in the future. But maybe he was also trying to warn me about my powers manifesting, about what I could do, and what I could potentially do if the wrong creature got ahold of my powers. Not that I'm even sure what my powers are. All that's happened so far is I've seen the death of others and seen visions of blood painting the land.

"That's one of my theories." Jax grips the wheel as we

drive over a bump in the road, his gaze darting back to the trees. He visibly stiffens, his muscles raveling into knots, and making me wonder where in the heck we're going, and why he seems so tense about it. "But that's just one of them. There are a few other possibilities."

"Like what?" When I notice him stiffen even more, I decide it's time for him to fess up as to where we're going. "Dude, where the crap are we? Because you look super tense, even for you." I grin at my clever remark, but my lips tip downward as Jax's knuckles turn white from gripping the steering wheel so tightly. "Okay, for reals, where are we?"

He hesitates. "We're in pixie territory."

Right as he says it, the trees open up and the road flattens out, giving me a view of a gated entryway that arches toward the glittering purple sky.

Wait... glittering purple sky?

"Um... why's the sky purple?" I slant forward and tilt my head to get a better view.

"Well..." He parks in front of the entryway, shoves the shifter into park, and shuts off the engine. A frown forms on his lips as he assesses the gate. Then with a sigh, he twists to face me. "So, a handful of days after Ollie left, I received a message from him. He'd found a pixie that was going to lead him into Hushing Forest, but, like all pixies, he said she was a little bit sketchy. So we both agreed that if I didn't hear from him within a week or so, that I was to come here, go to a bar called The Wandering Glitter Seekers, and find a pixie named Jessa. That she'd know where Ollie is."

"Okay." Confusion tap dances through me. "Why haven't you told me about this until now? And where is this place even?" I gesture at the glittery purple sky.

"I didn't tell you because I was worried that if something happened to me..." He lets out an exhale.

"That I'd go here by myself?" I ask, and he shrugs, avoiding my gaze. I shake my head, irritation biting under my skin. "Okay, wolf boy, let's get something straight right now." I square my shoulders. "In no way, shape, or crazy vampire am I ever going to be the kind of person that needs to be protected. I need to make my own decisions based on all the facts. So you need to give me all the facts. I mean it, Jax." I narrow my eyes at him so he knows I mean business. "Don't keep shit from me to try to protect me." I stick out my pinkie. "In fact, pinkie swear you won't. And when we have the time, we can turn the pinkie promise into a blood promise."

The corners of his lips twitch as he glances at my pinkie. Then he meets my gaze and hitches his pinkie with mine. "All right, violet eyes, you have yourself a deal."

Again, I'm thrown off balance by how easily he agrees. But I'll worry about that later. Right now, I need to figure out where this place is, because the fact that he's been avoiding telling me has me questioning just how dangerous it is.

"Good." I unhitch my pinkie from his. "Now tell me where we are."

He gives a short pause before reluctantly saying, "We're at the entrance to the pixie realm."

ALANA

At first, I think I've heard him wrong. Because the entrance to the pixie realm...

I shake my head. "That's not possible. The only way into another realm is through a portal."

He arches a brow. "Who says we didn't go through a portal?"

I cock my brow right back at him. "I've seen my fair share of portals opened, so I know we didn't."

"I didn't say we opened one," he clarifies. "I just said we went through one."

Okay... "So you're saying that there's just some random portal in the forest back there," I point behind us. "And that basically anyone can just walk into the pixie realm?"

While I don't think Jax is much of a liar, I'm not sure if I believe him.

If there were a portal to the pixie realm in a place that anyone could walk into, wouldn't I have heard about it, seeing as how my parents are keepers and usually know those sorts of things?

He unfastens his seatbelt. "You have to have paranormal blood in your veins to go through it."

"Oh." I guess that makes sense. But what doesn't is... "How did you know it exists?"

"I've made a lot of connections while working cases—it's part of the job. And some of those connections happen to be pixies, who can get really chatty when they've had a glass or two of wine."

"Have you ever dated a pixie?" I ask, then mentally bitch slap myself.

Why in the heck did I just ask that?

A smirk curls across his lips. "Would you be jealous if I had?"

I roll my eyes. "No. I was just curious."

"Sure you were." He grins. "And for the record, I haven't dated a pixie." He chews on his bottom lip, looking at me way too intently. "Have you?"

I snort a laugh. "Hell no."

His brow lifts. "Are you prejudice against pixies or something?"

"No. I've just never dated anyone."

"*Ever?*"

"Nope."

Curiosity flickers across his face. "Have you ever kissed anyone before?"

I roll my eyes. "Not that it's any of your business, but yeah, I have. I just haven't dated anyone."

Surprise flickers in his eyes and my jaw ticks.

Why does he seem so surprised by this?

"Stop acting surprised. I know I annoy the hell out of you, but some guys like my sparkling personality." I smile haughtily. "And it's not like I haven't had the opportunity to date. I've just spent a lot of my life caught up in the keeper's world and didn't even try to date." I move to get out of the car. "And FYI, I don't know why you're acting like you're a player. Dash told me you rarely date." As soon as I mention Dash, I regret my words. "I'm sorry. I shouldn't have brought him up."

He presses his lips together, pausing for a second. "You're fine. Besides, he's technically still sort of alive. Well, at least I'm going to assume so until proven otherwise." He looks away from me as he scoots to the edge of the seat to get out. But then he pauses and glances over his shoulder at me. "I'm not annoyed by your personality, Alana. That's not why I acted surprised that you've never dated anyone. It's just that... It's kind of hard to believe that you never have."

"I already told you why I haven't."

"I know, but..." He hesitantly chews on his bottom lip.

"But what?" I press. When he doesn't answer, I let out a frustrated groan. "Dude, we've got to work on you not finishing your sentences."

The corners of his lips quirk. "I'm just being cautious with my words."

I lift a brow. "Why?"

He shrugs. "So I don't piss you off."

I resist a frown, but I'm concerned.

Since when does he worry about pissing me off?

"Are you sure everything's okay?" I ask for probably the thousandth time.

He nods. "Of course." Then he ducks out of the car and closes the door, moving so quickly that I wonder if he's trying to escape something.

But the only thing around is me, so...

Am I what he's trying to escape?

ALANA

As I'm getting out of the car, I notice my sprite bite is starting to reappear, so I slather a bit of fey magicae onto to it to keep the side effects from reappearing. Then I hide the bag underneath the seat, knowing I can't risk the bag getting stolen, since Jayse hasn't tracked down the sprite who bit me yet, so he can extract some pixie dust from it. It's the only cure to my bite, and if he can't get the pixie dust, I'm so screwed. Like I'll-turn-into-a-giggling-stupid-obnoxious-sprite kind of screwed.

Once the bite's effects are sedated, I put on an ankle holster and slip a knife into it, per Jax's suggestion, although I would've done it anyway.

Jax waits for me outside of the car while I do all of this, and I can tell he's avoiding me. I have no idea why, but I add it to the list I'm creating of things he's done that are out of character for him.

After I'm good and ready to go, I hop out of the car. "Let's get this show on the road," I tell Jax.

He doesn't respond, his silver eyes skimming across the pair of clunky boots I put on, along my legs that are visible from the shorts I'm wearing. He scrolls across every inch of me until his gaze collides with mine.

"Why are you inspecting me?" I ask, crossing my arms. "Worried I forgot to put the knife in my holster? Because FYI, that'd never happen. I'm a pro when it comes to being prepared for danger." I wink at him.

He almost smiles, but then tears his gaze off me and strides up the path, muttering, "Follow me."

"Okay, then." I follow after him, wondering why he suddenly has a stick up his ass.

As we get close to the entrance, he suddenly slams to a halt, grabs my arm, and stops me.

"Before we go in, I want to stress how important it is that no one knows who you are." He looks me straight in the eye as he lowers his voice. "I don't even want you giving anyone your real last name. This is pixie territory, and you can't trust anyone here."

I give him a salute. "Yes, boss, sir."

He smashes his lips together, a soft groan reverberating from his chest. "Such a smartass," he mumbles as he releases my arm.

Then he takes off up the dirt path again, leaving me to rush after him.

"And you're such a grumpy werewolf," I remark as I jog to catch up with him.

He heaves out an exhale, slowing to a stop in front of the gated entryway.

The locked gated entryway, I might add.

"So how do we get in?" I ask as I stop beside him.

He flips open a hidden latch on the gate and punches in a passcode.

Okay, so he's been here before.

As the gates open up, he tosses me an arrogant smirk. "Try not to be too impressed."

"I'm not, since it's pretty clear you've been here before."

"Once or twice," he replies as he steps through the entrance.

I trail after him, trying not to let my jaw hit the cobblestone pavement paving the path through the quaint town. But it's difficult to conceal my shock.

I've never really been to another realm before, and the magic sprinkled all over the stone buildings, and the neon flowers and trees, is breathtaking. So is the violet shimmer casting across everything. But I manage to rein back on my shock as I note several pixies wandering up and down the jeweled sidewalks.

Pixies, while dangerous, are beautiful creatures that come in all different shapes and sizes. Purple, shimmering skin, blue, glittering eyes, sparkling pink hair; I can see at least a dozen with those features. And the attire they wear is as glittery and bright as the town.

"This is..." I shake my head in astonishment. "Magical."

Jax observes me from the corner of his eye. "You act like you've never been to another realm before."

"I haven't," I admit as we stroll up the path, walking past shops, bars, and stores, all the titles containing words like *glitter* and *shimmering* in them.

"Really? Because I thought with you growing up in the keeper world, you would've realm traveled a lot."

"Nah. A lot of Keepers don't want their kids traveling until they get their keeper mark and their keeper power."

"That makes sense, I guess." He grows quiet, stepping closer to me.

"How much have you realm traveled?" I wonder.

He gives a half-shrug. "Quite a bit."

"Is that a werewolf thing?"

"No, it's my family's thing." He rakes his fingers through his hair, making the strands go askew. "My father traveled a lot to obtain his collection of powerful objects that I told you about. And when Dash and I were younger, he'd take us with him. But he stopped taking Dash after we discovered his powers. And then I got older and... things happened. So that was the end of my family's travels. But I've traveled on my own since then."

I'm not sure what to say to that. According to Dash, their father isn't a good guy. But Jax has denied this. That's understandable, though. Even when my grandfather looked extremely guilty of committing terrible crimes, I refused to accept it. And maybe Jax and Dash's father really isn't a bad guy. I've never met him before, so I have hardly anything to judge it on other than what Jax and Dash have told me. But what I do know is that usually when someone is collecting powerful objects, it's not just to have them on display. That usually there's a darker reason behind it.

"I really need to get a hold of my dad," Jax mumbles as he digs his phone out of his pocket. Then he frowns. "Great. We're out of signal."

I'm not surprised since we just entered another realm.

I mean, does the pixie realm even have cell service?

I don't ask, not wanting to look like even more of a

tourist than I already do. I also bite down on my tongue to avoid saying anything about Jax's father.

But when Jax had first suggested we turn to his father for help, I'd verbalized my reluctance about it and that had led to a mild argument. So, I've decided that for now, I'll keep my opinions to myself, which might be a first. But I kind of have to be this way about this since Jax is one of the few that stood by me when I insisted my grandfather was innocent.

"So where is this bar located?" I change the subject, becoming highly aware that almost all of the pixies nearby are staring at us.

He pockets his phone and glances around at the shops lining the street. "If I'm remembering correctly, it's just a few more streets up."

I nod, holding the gaze of one of the pixies staring at me, hoping to make them uneasy enough that they'll look away. But nope. They just smirk at me. I should've known better. Pixies are cocky little a-holes.

"I stand out too much," I tell Jax, gesturing at my black t-shirt, shorts, and the plaid shirt tied around my waist. Then I motion at his grey shirt and black jeans. "So do you." I lower my hand. "Maybe we should stop in one of these stores and buy new outfits."

"It wouldn't help," he says, giving me a once over. "We'd still need to be covered in glitter, have pointy ears, and a crazy hair color."

"We could always roll in some glitter." I smile amusedly at the idea of Jax rolling around in glitter like a dog. "I'm sure you'd be good at that."

He rolls his eyes. "If you're making dog jokes again, then I'm going to start making jokes about your violet eyes."

I make a big show of rolling my eyes. "Go ahead. I've heard it all before."

His forehead creases. "Creatures tease you about your eyes?"

I shrug. "When I was younger, yeah. Kids used to call them creepy freaky. It stopped, though, when I got older."

A trace of a smile pulls at his lips, but he doesn't say anything.

"What's that look for?" I playfully nudge him in the side with my elbow.

He shakes his head. "It's nothing."

"No, clearly it's something, or else you wouldn't have done one of your very rare smiles." I cross my arms. "So fess up. What is it?"

He meets my gaze, and amusement is glittering in his eyes, which is a strange look for him. "I was just thinking that you probably stopped getting teased when you got older because creatures realized that your eyes, while freaky," he smirks, and I give him a dirty look, "Are actually really pretty."

I stare at him unimpressed. "Seriously? My eyes are really pretty? Again, let me repeat: what the heck is going on with you?"

His smile promptly fades. "And again, let me repeat, nothing's going on with me other than I'm risking my ass to protect yours. You're welcome, by the way."

"And there's the cocky wolf boy." I grin. "I was wondering how long he was gonna stay asleep."

"Well, he wanted to stay asleep for a bit longer, but some loudmouth wouldn't let him," he quips.

I slowly start to feel on balance again and realize how off balance I'd felt.

So weird.

I don't have too much time to overanalyze that, though, as Jax comes to a stop in front of an iridescent building with rainbow-tinted windows and a bright ass pink door. Sparkling above the crystallized dome roof is a flashing spritz of magic that reads: *The Wandering Glitter Seekers.*

"This is the bar we're going to?" I have to work hard not to gape like a tourist.

I don't do a very great job, though, since Jax has to reach over and push my mouth shut.

"I know. It's very flashy," he says as he fishes his phone out to glance at the screen again.

"Yeah, flashy is a total understatement." I watch in awe as fireworks blaze from the magical sign. "This place looks like someone barfed up rainbows and pixie dust all over it."

Jax chuckles but then sighs as he stuffs his phone into his pocket.

"Still no signal, huh?" I ask and he shakes his head.

"No. My phone went off a couple of times right before we went through the portal, but that's it. And those messages weren't from my father. They were from the school..." He gives a hesitant pause. "And from Vivianne."

"*What?*" I cry out way too loudly and draw more attention to us. I lower my voice and lean closer to him. "Why the heck did she message you?"

"Because she wants to know if I have any idea where you are." He massages the back of his neck tensely. "Apparently, you not showing up for your classes this morning has some creatures concerned. It probably doesn't help that no one's really seen you since they found that dead witch in your room."

"Shit, I didn't even think about that," I mumble. "I hope they haven't called my parents. I don't want them to worry. It's why I haven't called them yet and told them about what's going on."

"Well, you might want to when we leave the portal, just in case someone from the school does call them."

"I need to call them now... Maybe I have a signal even though you don't. You never know." I reach for my pocket to get my phone out and check, but he captures my arm, stopping me.

"Even if you do, you can't make that call out here." He gives me a pressing look. "The last thing you want is to risk a creature from here overhearing that conversation."

"Yeah, good idea—" I stumble backwards as a tall pixie with flowing lavender hair pushes by me.

"Watch it freak," she sneers, elbowing me in the side.

My fingers ball into fists. *Don't punch her, Alana. She's a pixie and can curse you if she wants to.*

"Freak? Wow, that's clever," I smart off to her. "How long did it take you to come up with that one?"

She narrows her emerald eyes at me, but then her lips tug into a smirk. "Just you wait." She smooths her hands over her hair, spins around, and strolls toward the side of the bar.

"Are all pixies that bitchy?" I ask, stretching out my fingers.

Jax scratches at his tattooed arm. "Yeah, but..." He glances at me with concern. "That was a little weird."

"Nah." I dismiss him with a wave of my hand. "Remember what I told you in the car? I've been called a freak many times."

"Still, I'm a bit worried. With…" He flicks a nervous glance around, then leans in, his wolfish, earthy scent flooding my nostrils. "Everything we've discovered about you, we need to be cautious."

"Yeah, but no one but you and me know about that," I remind him. "Well, and the—"

He places his finger to my lips and gives me a warning look. "Remember the number one rule about that name."

"Right." My lips move against his finger. "Sorry. Rookie mistake."

He jerks his hand away from my mouth and pulls a face.

"Hey, I don't have cooties," I joke, but he doesn't even so much as crack a smile.

Typical werewolf. Always taking everything so seriously. I'm just glad he's acting like his uptight self again.

"I don't think you have cooties. You just got spit on my hand." Then he makes a big show of wiping off his hand on the side of his pants while making a repulsed face.

I roll my eyes. "It's just a little spit. Stop being such a drama queen."

"I will when you learn not to drool so much."

"Well, you'd be the expert on that, wolf boy."

"Yeah, I am." His eyes darken. "So here's some advice from an expert. Learn how to swallow your saliva instead of letting it fall out of your mouth because a lot of people are going to be repulsed by it."

"I didn't drool on you. You're just exaggerating."

"Tell that to my wet hand. And the wet spot on my pants."

"Why? Did you piss in them or something?"

He gapes at me. "Did you seriously just ask me if I pissed my pants?"

I give an innocent shrug. "You're the one that stressed how wet they are."

He leans in toward me. "Yeah, because you drooled on me."

I roll my eyes again. "I didn't drool on you."

When he only smirks, frustration bubbles through me.

I stand on my tiptoes and lick his neck. "There. Now you really do have my drool all over you." I slant back, putting on my best shit-eating grin.

But when I catch sight of the tension in his expression and the intensity flashing in his eyes, my smile falters.

"Relax. I was just messing with you." I reach out to wipe my drool off his neck, but he snatches hold of my wrist.

"Don't touch me," he bites out, moving my hand away.

I glare at him. "What the heck is wrong with you? I was just messing around."

"Yeah, well..." He starts mumbling incoherently under his breath before spinning on his heels. "Wait right here. I'll be back." Then he storms off toward the side of the building, leaving me standing in front of the bar on my own, feeling confused and kind of pissed off.

Yeah, I licked his neck, but I was joking around. And I thought he was too, but apparently not.

Well, Alana, you did want him to go back to his normal, brooding self.

But this is a whole new level of brooding. In fact, I've

never seen him get that riled up except for maybe when vampires tried to attack me. He may say nothing is going on with him, but something definitely is. And the last time he acted this out of character was because he was possessed.

I gulp. Wait. Did he somehow become possessed again? If so, who's possessing him? That stupid witch named Pinkie? Or someone else?

It doesn't make any sense, though. No one else has been around us for a while. But if he's not possessed then what in the crap is going on with him—

A hand slaps down over my mouth. Then I feel someone move up behind me.

"Now where's your smartass remarks," a female voice whispers in my ear.

It takes me a second to place the voice, but I manage to get there. The pixie who told me, "just you wait."

I'm about to kick her in the shin and elbow her in the stomach when a blast of glitter showers over me.

My eyes roll into the back of my head as exhaustion sweeps through my veins.

Sleeping glitter... She sprayed sleeping glitter all over me...

Crap, I'm definitely in deep trouble, is the last thought I have before everything goes dark.

JAX

I LOWER MY FOREHEAD TO THE WALL AND PRESS MY fists against it, the rough surface scraping my knuckles. "Get your shit together," I mumble. "You can't let her find out you're bonded to her. She'll freak out and leave if she does."

And Alana can't be on her own right now. Not with so much danger surrounding her. She probably needs more protection than I can give her, but since we can't trust anyone at the moment, it has to be just her and me.

Her and me. I shake my head. My wolf likes the sound of that way too much. Just like he liked her licking me way too much.

It had been bad enough when her lips brushed against my finger after I placed my finger over her mouth. I'd almost lost control then but managed to play it off by teasing her. But then she had to go and lick me, and I damn near kissed her. I can only imagine what would've happened if I had. She probably would've slapped me, maybe even took off.

Then we'd have drawn even more attention, and that's the last thing we need.

What I need is to find a way to break the bond between us. I've heard of ways to do so, but it's always been for breaking the bond a creature has with a werewolf, not the other way around. And since I'm not positive how I became bonded to Alana instead of her being bonded to me, I'm not sure how to break the bond. But I'll find a way, even if my wolf isn't completely on board.

After breathing in and out several times, I get my wolf to simmer down. Then I push away from the wall and head back to Alana. When I round the corner of the bar, though, she isn't standing where I left her.

"Where the hell did she go?" I mutter as I turn in a circle, my gaze sweeping across the nearby shops and the sidewalks.

Several pixies are roaming around with bags in their hands, appearing to mind their own business. But the fact that not a single one of them is gawking at me has me more on edge than when they were openly staring.

Something's going on...

As a shorter pixie with chin-length green hair and silver eyes passes by me, not making eye contact, I snag hold of the sleeve of her shirt.

"Have you seen my friend?" I ask, my gaze boring into her. "She was standing out here just a few minutes ago."

"Why the hell would I have seen her?" she sneers. "I don't pay attention to humans."

I arch a brow. "I never said she was human."

She tries to yank her arm away from me, but I tighten my grip.

"Let go of me, wolf," she snaps, jerking her arm again.

But I only hold on tighter. "I'll let you go when you tell me where she is," I growl, feeling my bones starting to shift.

Shit. If I'm not careful, I'll shift into my wolf. And it's not even a full moon. Not that this would be the first time that happened. It happened the other day when I was possessed. But I'm not possessed now. Apparently, though, being able to shift without a full moon has remained even after the possession has worn off.

Just like my wolf's bond to Alana remains.

It has me worried. With all these experiments being done by the Electi, did they somehow manage to do one on me?

I really need to find someone who can tap into my mind and find out what memories are hidden in there.

Yeah, if only it were that easy. But with everything else on my plate, and with me being unsure who I can trust, I'm not positive how to go about doing that. Alana has suggested that maybe her aunt who's a witch can help us, but I'm not sure I want to involve Alana's family in this. If we do, we could be putting them in danger—anyone who knows about the Electi is in danger. Like Dash. I don't know for sure what happened to him, but I have an unsettling feeling it might have to do with him knowing about the Electi.

"Your eyes..." The pixie murmurs. "How are you shifting when it's not a full moon?"

I take a deep breath, close my eyes, then open them again. "I'm not shifting," I manage to say evenly. "Now take me to the girl that was out here or else I'm going to squeeze your arm hard enough to break bones."

Her nostrils flare. "You werewolves think you're so

much better than the rest of us. Well, newsflash, even being a wolf isn't going to save your precious girlfriend."

I don't even bother correcting her about Alana not being my girlfriend, for several messed up reasons. Instead, I constrict my grip on her arm until I feel the bones start to splinter apart.

Her face contorts in pain. "All right, I'll take you to her!" she cries out.

I loosen my grip. "Then lead the way."

Gritting her teeth, she stomps forward toward the entrance to the bar. But she doesn't go inside, instead veering around to the side and down an alleyway. She continues down it until we reach a crystallized door nestled at the back.

"You better not try anything," I warn as she reaches for the doorknob. "Or else you'll end up with worse than a broken arm."

"Whatever," she mumbles as her fingers wrap around the door handle. "You'll regret this."

I squeeze her arm in a warning, and she glares at me as she jerks open the door.

On the other side is a narrow hallway lined with mirrors that lead to a pearl-white door.

"What is this place?" I ask as we step inside, the mirrors instantly giving me vertigo.

"The princess's private room," the pixie replies, her heels clicking against the glittering ruby floor. "She comes to the bar a lot and as a thank you, the owner gave her a private room."

The pixie princess? The princess of the pixies took Alana?

Shit, this is bad. Very, very bad.

JAX

It takes me a moment to completely process what the pixie said. Then questions start swarming my thoughts. Why in the hell would the princess of the pixies want Alana? Unless she's working with the fey princess, aka Vivianne, at least I'm ninety-nine percent sure that's who the fey princess is. What I'm not sure about, though, is why the pixie princess would be working with the fey princess? From what I understand, fey and pixies don't get along very well.

But perhaps word has gotten around about this war that's supposed to be lingering in the future and groups are now pairing up. Still, why would they want Alana? That is, unless they know about her powers. But since even I'm not exactly sure of everything Alana can do, how would anyone else know?

Unless they have a connection to the Electi.

Worry stirs through me. Is someone from the Electi waiting on the other side of that door? Is the pixie princess part of their group?

"What does the princess want with my friend?" I try to get some answers as we arrive in front of the door.

"Friend, huh?" the pixie muses with a smirk. "If she's just a friend, then why can I smell how much you like her every time you say her name?"

I grind my teeth, loathing how right she is. It's a curse of being a werewolf. Our scent manifests when we're nearby or thinking of someone we're attracted to. It's why Alana can smell a woodsy, earthy scent every time I'm near her. Even the first night I met her, that stupid scent made an appearance. Luckily, though, she hasn't caught onto that yet.

"Just open the damn door." I shove the pixie toward the door, on the brink of losing my composure.

She smirks, thrilled that she's pissing me off.

I take a deep breath, trying to get myself to calm down. "Open the door," I say in a more composed tone.

She rolls her eyes, but rotates the doorknob and pushes the door open.

On the other side is a dimly lit room with black walls lined with cushioned benches. Dangling from the ceiling are crimson chandeliers and sheer red curtains that drape around a platform. And lying in the middle of the platform is Alana, her eyes shut, her lips slightly parted. For a mind-losing moment, I think she's dead. But then I see her chest rise and fall as she takes a breath.

"What the hell did you do to her?" I growl, gripping the pixie's arm.

"I didn't do anything." She jerks her arm away from me. "The princess did."

I lean in her face. "Well, you can tell your princess to—"

"To what?"

I'm cut off by a female voice.

I look away from the pixie, my gaze falling to a figure emerging from the shadows of the room. Her dark red hair flows to the floor along with the green dress she's wearing. Her skin nearly matches the dress, and her eyes are as red as her hair.

And behind her are two male pixies, decked out in hideous sparkling outfits, her guards I'm assuming. But they don't look that intimidating. Not that I'm going into this with that mentality.

No, I need to be on alert.

"You're not going to finish that threat?" the princess says after a beat of silence stretches by. "Such a shame. I always look forward to meeting creatures who are bold enough to threaten me. It gives me the opportunity to torture them."

The crystals on the chandelier clink as silence stretches by again, and I attempt to figure out the best way to approach this situation. Should I threaten her? Let myself shift and hope my wolf handles this for me? Probably not, since my wolf will more than likely try to bite Alana. Not in a violent way, but to bond himself to her even more.

I'm still attempting to figure out what to do when the princess busts up laughing.

"I'm just kidding," she declares. "But the look on your face is priceless."

Um... What?

Seriously, what the hell is going on?

"I'm sorry," the princess says, dabbing tears from her eyes. "I'm sure you're confused, and it's probably very rude of me to laugh."

"Yeah, it is," I agree. "So why don't you tell me what's going on? And why in the hell you took my friend?"

"Friend, huh?" she muses with her head angled to the side. "Funny, because I swear I can sense a bond between the two of you."

I shake my head, pretending to be calmer than I feel. But the last thing I need is for the pixie princes to find out I'm bonded to Alana. "No, you can't."

"My mistake," she says amusedly. She remains quiet for an unnerving moment before gesturing at one of the benches. "Please have a seat, Jax. There's some things I'd like to discuss with you."

"How do you know my name?" I ask, assessing her closely.

She rubs her lips together. "Because your friend Oliver told me."

"You've talked to Ollie?" I realize my mistake as soon as I say it.

It's never a good idea to let a pixie know they have more information than you. They'll use it against you if they get the opportunity.

A smile spreads across her lips. "Who do you think told him the location of Hushing Forest?"

So this is the pixie who told Ollie where to go? Jessa, I think her name is. But he never mentioned in the message he sent me that she was the princess of the pixies.

Shit, Ollie, what have you gotten yourself into?

I'm almost positive Ollie had to trade something in order to get the location to Hushing Forest. And making a trade with the princess of pixies...

Yeah, I'm really worried about him.

"You don't need to be worried," she reassures me. "Your friend is all right. In fact, he's in excellent hands right now."

I smash my lips together as irritation simmers under my flesh. "Where is he?"

"Unfortunately, I can't tell you that," she says. I'm about to lose my cool when she adds, "However, I can tell you about what you came here looking for."

Confusion spins through me. What does she know?

"I'm referring to your... friend." She says *friend* as if it's amusing. "And what she is."

I swallow the lump that wedges into my throat. How does she know about Alana? Did Ollie tell her about Alana's abilities? Why would he do that? He should know how dangerous doing that is.

"Don't worry, your friend didn't tell me anything," she clarifies as if she can read my mind.

I'd be worried she can except pixies don't have that kind of power. No, their abilities lie more in the direction of manipulation.

I need to keep my lips shut so I don't accidentally get lured into a trap.

The princess lets out a quiet sigh. "Please have a seat, and I'll try to answer some of your questions."

I shake my head, my gaze flicking to Alana. "I'm not sitting down until I can check on her."

The princess gives a nod. "Very well. Let's wake your friend up, shall we?"

She sweeps the curtains out of the way before stepping onto the platform Alana is lying on. Then the princess reaches into her pocket and sprinkles a bit of sparkling dust across Alana's body. Within seconds, Alana's eyes open, and she sucks in a huge breath of air.

My wolf slightly calms down.

She's okay.

"Take a deep breath, my dear," the princess tells Alana as she frantically looks around the room.

Only when her gaze finds me does she settle down a little bit. I feel a bit of pride over being able to calm her down. But again, I'm not sure if it's my wolf reacting that way or me.

Once Alana gets her breathing under control, she hops off the platform and reaches for the knife tucked in her ankle holster.

"Don't," I warn, carrying her gaze, pleading for her to listen to me for once.

If she withdraws that knife, all hell will break loose. And I want to get some answers before that happens.

Thankfully, for once, she listens to me. Although, she looks pissed off, her jaw ticking as she stands back up without taking out her knife.

"Smart choice," the princess tells her, eliciting a glare from Alana. The princess chuckles. "You two are amusing." Then she whisks over to the bench and takes a seat, waiting for us to join her.

I trade a look with Alana then make my way over to the princess and sit down. Alana begrudgingly follows, sitting beside me, her cotton candy scent engulfing my nostrils and sending my wolf into a frenzy. She's smelled like that ever since I met her and it's always made my wolf go a bit crazy. But the bond has upped the craziness.

Calm the hell down, I tell him. *Before someone notices.*

Apparently, though, I don't get him composed quickly enough, and the princess gives me a knowing look.

I glare at her and Alana notices, her gaze bouncing between the two of us.

"Okay, someone tell me what the hell is going on," Alana demands, crossing her arms and staring me and the princess down. "Because the last thing I can remember is some bitchy pixie knocked me out with some sleeping dust. And then I wake up here." She glances around the room with her brows furrowed, "Wherever here is. And I don't know who any of you are, yet Jax seems to."

"You're in my private room," the princess explains. "And I'm the princess of the pixies and these are my guards." She points at the male pixies then her gaze slides to me, her lips quirking. "And your *friend* doesn't know us."

"Okaaay," Alana drags out the word, glancing at me, hoping for more of an explanation.

"I'm not sure what's going on either," I inform her. "Other than she says she knows Ollie. I'm not sure why she knocked you out, though." I glance at the princess with my brows raised.

"Oh, that was for my personal entertainment," she explains with a flick of her wrist. "I sometimes get bored, so when we have visitors, I use that as an opportunity for entertainment."

I'm not sure if she's lying, but I decide to focus on the bigger problem.

I cross my arms. "What do you know about what Ollie was looking for?"

A trace of a smile appears on her lips. "I know that he was looking for the Scrawl of Secrets so he could help a friend identify a rare creature." Her gaze skates to Alana and I stiffen. "He seemed desperate enough that I decided to help him, but not without getting a little bit of entertainment out of it."

"You seem really big on that," I say, my tone laced with suspicion.

"Like I said, I can get quite bored," she replies, her red eyes glittering. "Which is why I made a deal with Oliver." She rests back in the bench, crossing her legs and adjusting her dress.

Then she grows quiet, smiling to herself, and I feel like I'm being baited.

"What deal?" I decide to take the bait.

"That's between Oliver and me," she replies. "What I want to discuss with you is the deal you're going to make with me to get the Scrawl of Secrets.

"Do you have it?" Alana asks with that snarky bite in her tone that I both love and hate. "Or are you just trying to play us?"

The princess taps her finger against her lips. "Now why would you think I'd do something that?"

"Um, let me think," Alana replies with sarcasm dripping her tone. "Maybe because you had me knocked out and taken here so you could lure Jax here. At least that's what I'm assuming. The question, though, is why? Because I'm not buying into this whole bullshit entertainment reason."

I sneak Alana a warning look. *"You're pushing it too far,"* I mouth.

She shakes her head and mouths, *"No, I'm not."*

That stubborn woman. She can drive me insane sometimes, something my wolf seems to like since he begins to stir inside me, purring awake, and begging me to bite her.

The princess grins at me. "And this is why I've brought you here."

Alana looks at me confusedly.

I shrug, just as perplexed. "I don't know what she means any more than you do."

"He actually doesn't," the princess tells her. "Not really, anyway." She glances at her guards then back at me. "I want to make a deal. I'll give you the Scrawl of Secrets, and in exchange for my silence, you'll give me a bit of entertainment."

I don't like where this is going. "Your silence about what?"

A smirk pulls at her lips. "About what she is." She flits a glance at Alana, and suddenly, I can see it.

She knows.

Alana stiffens, and I clench my hands into fists, fighting the urge to silence the princess right here and now.

"How do you know what she is?" I ask in a low tone, measuring the princess's reaction.

I expect her to say she looked it up in the scrawl, but that's not the response she gives.

"There's a rumor going around about a rare creature with deadly gifts. She has eyes like violets, the beauty of a siren, and is completely clueless about what she is. And from what Ollie told me, I figured out that he was looking for an answer for this rare creature. And when Alana showed up here with her violet eyes and beauty that can make werewolves go mad," she throws me a smirk and I glower at her, "I put two and two together."

I exchange a look with Alana, who's gone very pale.

"Who's looking for me?" she asks quietly. "And why?"

The princess shrugs, but I get the feeling she's lying.

"I'm not sure. All I can offer is an answer to what you are." She crooks a finger at her guards.

The shorter of the two steps forward, sticks his hand into his jacket pocket, and retrieves a small, leather-bound book with *Scrawls of Secrets* engraved in gold ink across the front.

I straighten at the sight of it. "Where the hell is Ollie?" I snap at the princess.

"I already told you he's being taken care of," she replies vaguely as she takes the book from the guard. "And that's all I'm going to tell you or else I risk you searching for him. And right now, I can't let that happen."

My lips part, ready to demand for her to tell me, but she lifts her hand, silencing me.

"Let it drop or else I won't give you this," she warns, holding up the book.

My claws begin to slip out from my knuckles, but I mentally will them back.

Don't lose control, Jax. Try to handle this situation in a non-violent way first.

"You promise Ollie's safe?" I ask through gritted teeth.

She nods, setting the book onto her lap. "You have my oath that he is."

I relax a bit. A pixie's oath is one of the very few ways you can get the truth out of them. "Okay."

She grins. "Now that we've got that settled, it's time to make our bargain."

Alana lets out a frustrated groan. "Goddamn pixies," she

mutters under her breath. "I'd like to take their glitter and stuff it up their asses."

I bite back a smile, but keep my attention on the princess. "What do you want?"

"Oh, it's nothing major," the princess insists. "I simply want a kiss. That's it, and then you can have the Scrawl of Secrets."

"A kiss?" I state with skepticism. "That's all you want, and then you're just going to give us an ancient book that contains all of the info to almost every rare creature that's ever existed."

"Well, it's only a copy of the Scrawl of Secrets," she clarifies, holding up the book. "The real book contains a lot of secrets belonging to my kind. There's no way I can give you that one, so I'm offering you this copy that only contains the information I'm okay with you having. However, I assure you this one works the same way. It just has fewer pages. And it has the answer you're looking for about what Alana is."

"Why can't you just tell us then?" I question. "If you know what she is already?"

She shakes her head. "I've been spelled into silence. We all have."

Shock lashes through me. "By who?"

She shakes her head again with her lips fused together. "We've also been spelled never to speak his name."

My chest constricts. I have a suspicion she's talking about the leader of the Electi, which means they've probably been here.

Suddenly, making a bargain with the princess of the pixies seems like the least of our problems.

I start to rise to my feet. "Alana, we need to leave."

Her brows knit, but she starts to stand up anyway.

"Stop," the princess commands and her guards position themselves in front of the door.

"You think your sparkling guards can stop me?" I ask the princess in a low tone, a smirk spreading across my face.

She mirrors my smirk. "Don't let my guards' beauty fool you. They can be quite deadly when they need to be." When I roll my eyes, her smirk broadens. "My dear lovelies, show the werewolf what you can do."

I glance at the guards just in time to see their eyes cloud over. Then smoke begins to funnel through the room, moving like snakes toward us.

I wrap my arm around Alana's waist protectively and draw her toward me. "What is that?"

"Death smoke," the princess answers with a grin. "It's very toxic to all creatures. Well, except for demons."

My grip on Alana tightens, and I pull her toward me until her back is pressed against my chest. Normally, she probably would've put up a fight about me trying to protect her, but I think she might be in shock.

"But only demons can make that smoke," Alana says as the smoke slithers toward us.

"That's because my guards are demons," the princess says with pride. When we both gape at her, she shrugs. "What? Do you really think I'd let pixies protect me? My kind are way too fickle."

She's right, but what I don't understand is...

"How did you get demons to protect you?" I start coughing as the smoke reaches us. I know the drill. If we breathe in too much, the poison will make our lungs wither.

"Can you get them to turn off the smoke? We won't try to run."

"Wise choice." She snaps her fingers, and just like that, the smoke evaporates. She focuses on me again. "And as for your first question, I got the demons to protect me by making a bargain with them. Just like the fey have allied with the water fey and the vampires with the wolves. Right now, everyone needs as many allies as they can get. And the more powerful allies, the better."

"What are you talking about?" I say. "The wolves haven't sided with the vampires. I'd know if they had."

"Would you?" she questions. "Because from what I can sense, your wolf is currently very distracted."

I bite down on my tongue to keep from snapping at her.

"Why are groups allying with each other?" Alana asks as she steps away from me.

"To protect ourselves," the princess replies. "With so many creatures getting taken these days, the rumors of war floating around, and the fights breaking out... We all have to prepare ourselves. And the more allies you have, the more power you have. And everyone knows that the most powerful usually come out on top."

"Not always, though," Alana mumbles, and I wonder if she's thinking about her grandpa.

Not the one who was a foreseer, but her other grandfather, Stephan.

From what I've been told, the story goes that he was a power-hungry keeper that collected Death Walkers, which are very dangerous creatures. He did it so he could try to take over the world. But things didn't work out that way.

"But enough about war." The princess claps her hands. "Let's talk about the deal we're going to make."

I eye her over. "You said you just want a kiss, right?"

A grin gradually spreads across her lips. "Yes, that's it. Just a kiss."

I resist an eye roll, but I'm not surprised. Pixies are known for doing stuff like this.

"Who do you want one from? Me?" I point at Alana. "Or her?"

"You misunderstand me. I don't want a kiss. I want to see you two kiss." Her gaze dances between Alana and me, her eyes sparkling with wicked delight.

"No freakin' way." Alana immediately shakes her head. "Ask for something else."

I remain silent, my heart thundering in my chest, knowing more than likely the princess won't give us another deal.

Knowing that if I do kiss Alana, I might lose control of my bond to Alana.

And honestly, I'm wondering if that's exactly what the princess is hoping for.

The question is: why?

ALANA

It seems like that's all I hear anymore. Talk of war. Sides pairing together. Sides eliminating each other. It makes the future seem doomed. But what I still don't understand is what part I play in all of this. And the answer could very well be in that book currently sitting on the pixie princess's lap. And all I have to do to get it is kiss Jax. And I should probably just do it. Suck up my pride. It's not like the kiss has to mean anything.

But I hate being told what to do.

"No freakin' way," I tell her, shaking my head.

Jax presses his lips together, his fingers curling into fists. I wait for him to protest too, but his lips remain shut, an unusual move for him.

The princess gives a shrug. "I guess we don't have a deal then, which means this conversation has now become a waste of my time." She starts to rise to her feet with the Scrawl of Secrets in her hand.

"Wait," Jax bites out.

I give him a *really* look.

He leans in and whispers, "We don't have a choice. She won't offer us another deal. It's not a pixie's MO."

He's right. I know he is. But it doesn't make the situation any less annoying.

"Fine," I grumble. "But after we leave this stupid sparkly hellhole and return to the human world, we're making a stop at a store so I can buy some mouthwash."

The corners of his lips twitch. "Fine, we can do that. Just like we can pretend that you're repulsed by the idea of kissing me."

I roll my eyes. "We both know that's not true. In fact, I'm pretty sure I might vomit right now."

His lips tug into a smirk. "Again, we can pretend."

My jaw ticks and my lips part with a snarky comeback. But then I decide to take the upper hand a different, standing on my tiptoes and sealing my lips to his. I mean, it's just a kiss. It doesn't have to mean anything. And I can make a big show of gagging afterward.

But as our lips brush, goosebumps sprout across my arms, a shiver trickling through my body.

Crap. I think I might kind of like kissing Jax.

That thought pixie kicks some sense into me, and I start to pull back. But Jax's lips chase mine, a groan reverberating through him. No, not a groan. A growl. Moments later, his teeth graze my bottom lip as he softly bites me. Just like he did when he was trying to bond me to him.

I jerk back, my eyelids snapping open.

"Your eyes are glowing," I whisper in horror, worried he's going to shift.

Jax's chest rises and crashes as he struggles to breathe

evenly. "I can't... I need to..." He starts to step toward me and holy hell fires, I think he's going to bite me.

And I can't let that happen even if it does kind of feel good.

I slam my hand against his chest. "Stop."

He freezes, blinking his eyes wildly. The glowing starts to subside as he gets his wolf under control.

I look him in the eye. "Are you good?"

He bobs his head up and down. "Yeah."

He still appears riled up, though, and I want to ask him what the hell is going on, but not here in front of the pixie princess who apparently has demons working for her.

Taking a deep breath, Jax spins around toward the princess and sticks out his hand. "You got your entertainment. Now give me the book."

She grins. "My suspicions are correct."

"Just give me the book," Jax growls out at the same time I say, "What suspicions?"

The princess locks gazes with Jax. "So she really doesn't know," she states, and Jax bares his fangs. But she ignores him, looking at me. "He's bonded to you."

A cold sensation spills through my veins. "What? No, he's not."

"I assure you he is. It's very rare for a wolf to become bonded to another creature. Usually, it's the other way around." Her brows knit. "But you're not really a creature, are you?"

I glance at Jax, looking for an explanation, but all he does is glare at the princess.

I fix my attention on the princess. "What do you mean, I'm not a creature? What else can I be?"

"Now what would be the fun in telling you? You're just lucky you're bonded to him, or I might try to keep you." With that, she hands Jax the book, gathers the bottom of her dress in her hand, and turns toward the guards. "I'm bored. Let's go check out some of the other clubs." She moves toward the door. "Take care, Alana. I'm sure we'll be seeing each other again." She waggles her fingers at me then waltzes out of the room, leaving behind a trail of confusion.

But I think that's what she intended to do.

ALANA

Jax and I barely speak during the journey back to his car. Not that I didn't try to talk to him. The moment we walked out of the princess's private room, I demanded an answer.

"You're bonded to me?" I'd hissed, shoving him hard enough to make him stumble.

He'd tucked the scrawl of secrets under his arm, cast a pressing look at the end of the alleyway where pixies are wandering then gritted through his teeth, "Not here."

I shook my head, fuming. "Whatever. I'll keep quiet for the five minute walk back to the car, but you're going to answer my question when we get there."

And that was the last verbal exchange we had, both of us sinking into unsettling silence as we power-walked back through the town and out the gates.

The instant we're safely in the car, though, I pull out my knife and point it at him. "You lied to me," I growl out.

He sets the book down on the console, then eyes the

knife, not appearing nearly as terrified as I want him to. "I didn't lie. I just omitted the truth."

"No, I flat out asked you if you were still bonded to me." I move the knife closer to him, but he doesn't even so much as flinch.

"No, you never did," he insists, twisting in the seat and starting up the engine.

I shake my head furiously. "It doesn't even matter if I did or didn't. You should've said something to me. With all the lies floating around..." I shake my head again, this time in disappointment. "You should've told me." And maybe I should've caught on. With how weird he was acting...

I should've known.

He meets my gaze, remorse flickering in his eyes. But who the hell knows if it belongs to him or his wolf. "I know I should've said something, but I was worried you'd freak out and try to run."

"So you what? Decided to keep it from me so you could try to keep me?" I snap, gripping the handle of the knife.

"No." He reaches for me, but then he withdraws back. "That's not what it was about. I was—and still am—worried about you being on your own... With everything going on... You need to be able to trust someone."

I let out a hollow laugh. "And that someone is supposed to be you?"

He nods, yanking his fingers through his hair. "I know I fucked up, but I swear I didn't keep this from you so I could have a hold of you. I just..." He sighs, his hand falling to his lap. "I just want you safe."

I think he might mean what he says, but still...

"You've been acting different... Nicer and it's weird. And

you almost shifted when I kissed you, so how can I know I'll be safe with you?" I position the knife in front of me again. "Maybe the best thing for me to do is to jump out of this car and run."

"I think deep down you know that's not true." He carries my gaze. "But if you want more proof, I'll give it to you." He sticks out his hand with his palm facing upward. "I think it's time to turn that pinkie promise into a blood promise."

I eye him over warily. "Are you being serious? Because if you do that, you're basically agreeing to tell me everything."

His gaze never wavers from mine. "I know what I'm getting into."

I don't lower the knife just yet. "Yeah, but is the bonded, overly nice Jax making the promise? Or is it the cocky Jax I first met?"

"Both," he replies then sighs. "Look, this whole bonded-to-you-thing... I'm going to try to find a way to reverse it. Because there's ways to reverse a creature from being bonded to a werewolf. I just need to find a way to do it when it's the opposite." He gives a short pause. "I just think that right now it's not our top priority."

I study him, attempting to tell if he's telling the truth or not. But he's always been a little difficult to read.

However, he is offering me a solution to that.

"Fine." I lower my knife, but only to cut open his palm.

He doesn't even so much as flinch as blood pools from his hand, but I detect the slightest bit of relief wash across his features.

Once his palm is good and bleeding, I slice open mine. Then I set the knife down and press my palm against his, choosing the words to the promise very carefully, since loopholes exist.

"*Promitto tibi non semper veritatem celare. Bene, ut diu ut praestabiles veritates exhiberet. Alii denique parvi manifesta sunt.*" My promise is pretty simple. That I'll always tell the truth to him and not keep secrets. But then I add on the stipulation of only important truths and secrets, and that having small secrets are okay. You know, just in case Jax tries to use the promise to get me to admit that I think he's hot.

He cracks a smile at my little addition and then repeats the promise to me.

Once we're done, I clean the blood off my hands and return the knife to my ankle holster.

"So are you keeping anything else from me?" I ask as he backs up the car and drives down the dirt road.

"No." He glances at me with his brow elevated. "How about you?"

I shake my head as I pick up the Scrawl of Secrets from off the console. It feels weird holding something so ancient that, from what the legend says, contains information about every magical creature that exists. Then again, it's only a copy.

"No important secrets on my part." I start to open the book. "Totally off the subject, but do you think Ollie is okay? I mean, why would he leave this with the pixie princess when it's pretty obvious she's not trustworthy. At least, that's what it seemed like to me."

He hesitates. "Honestly, since I have to be truthful, I should probably say that I don't think Ollie left that book with the princess."

"So how did she end up with it?"

"Well, I think she got it from him, but I doubt he gave it to her."

"So you what? Think the princess has him prisoner or something? Because if so, we need to go back and rescue him."

A weird look passes across his face. "You care about him enough to do that?"

"He's your friend, so yeah." I give a shrug, wondering why he's acting so weird about this.

"I know, but with what he is..." He chews on his lip, his gaze boring into me. "Most wouldn't want to try to save him."

"Ollie is a good guy," I say. "I don't care what he is."

He smiles at that. "You're a good person, Alana. You really are."

I point a finger at him. "No acting like a nice guy." I warn, my gaze lowering to the book. "It's too weird."

He chuckles. "Okay."

Shaking my head, I start to look back at the book. But my phone dings, distracting me.

I dig it out of my pocket, then blow out a relieved breath. "Well, I might have some good news."

His gaze skates to me "Really?"

I nod, swiping my finger across the screen. "While we were out of signal, I got a message from Thad."

"Put it on speaker," Jax tells me as I push play.

I do what he says and place the phone on the console. Moments later, Thad's voice flows from the speaker.

"Hey, Alana. Just returning your call." He gives a brief pause. "Look, all I can say about this thing with Dash is that you don't need to worry about him. He's okay."

"Thank Gods," Jax mumbles, releasing a loud exhale.

"He wants to meet up with you and Jax as soon as he can so he can explain some things, but he needs to lay low for a while," Thad continues. "I'll be in touch with you for him. Until then, you need to be careful. Stay clear of the academy, Vivianne, and Jax's and Dash's father. Dash says they can't be trusted, no matter what you think."

The line clicks as the message ends.

I pick up my phone and put it into my pocket, trying to measure up Jax's reaction.

He grips the steering wheel. "Why would Dash not want me to get in touch with my father? I know he doesn't like him, but still..." Moonlight flickers in his eyes as we cross over into the human world again, the purple sky shifting to a starry midnight blue.

"Maybe he knows something you don't," I suggest with caution. "I mean, clearly, he knows stuff about Vivianne."

"Yeah, but what exactly does he know about Vivianne?" His forehead crinkles in deep thought. Then his brow furrows as his phone rings. He reaches into his pocket and fishes it out.

Worry stirs inside me as I see *father* flash across the screen.

"Are you going to answer it?" I ask. If he does, I just might decide to try and run.

He hesitates before returning his phone to his pocket.

Silence skips by, and I let out a slow breath.

"That doesn't mean I don't trust my father," Jax says. "I'm just being careful... With the leader of the Electi possibly being a shapeshifter and all these creatures allying together, I just... I'm just being cautious." He says the latter more to himself.

"Cautious is good," I assure him.

He shrugs, growing quiet as he fixes his attention on the road.

And I focus on the Scrawl of Secrets, opening it all the way. "Why do you think the princess said I wasn't a creature?" I turn to the first page, but it's blank. "And why do you think she said she couldn't keep me because you're bonded to me."

"She was probably worried I'd shift is she tried to keep you. And then she'd have a werewolf running around in her town." He scratches at his forehead, tearing his gaze off the road, and looking at me. "As for the other part, I'm not sure. But the answer should be in that." He nods at the Scrawl of Secrets.

"Hopefully." I turn to the next page, but it's blank too. I frown, fanning through the pages, which are all blank. I'm about to say something when a piece of paper falls out of it. "What's this?" I pick it up and unfold it. Words are scribbled across it. "It's a letter to you from Ollie."

Jax doesn't seem that surprised. "What's it say?"

"*Jax,*" I start to read. "*If you're reading this, then it means you got the Scrawl of Secrets from the princess. You should know that she stole it from me after torturing me for hours. I didn't tell her anything, but she did have a foreseer dive into my mind, and she discovered why I was looking for the book. She also found a way to block my powers. I'm not sure how, though. She also knew about Alana before she captured me, so please be careful. Word is getting around about her, which means you're both in a lot of danger. You need to lay low for a while. I know you'll probably want to come looking for me after you read this note, but please don't. I'm headed back into Hushing Forest. I can't tell you why just yet, but it's for a good reason. But I am okay for now. When I can, I'll be in touch. Ollie."*

As soon as I finish reading the note, it lights on fire and withers into ash.

"He spelled the note," I state the obvious. "So at least we know we're the only ones who read it."

"I assumed as much." Jax scratches at his brow. "But why would he go back into the forest after he got the Scrawl of Secrets? Unless the princess made him. But again, why?"

"I'm not sure, but didn't it sound like he already had read through this book when he wrote the note and figured out what I am?"

"Yeah, it did." Jax glances at the book. "Maybe he went into the forest to protect what he discovered about you. I mean, I know the princess made it sound like he was doing something for her, but pixie's lie, so..."

"Yeah, I know. But why would he risk the dangers of the forest again just because he found out what I am? I mean, what's so important about me that needs to be kept a secret so badly?" Right as I say it, the pages of the book magically start to flip.

"It's charmed with magic," Jax explains as I gape at the book. "You asked the question, and now it's going to show you the answer."

"Just like that?"

"Pretty much."

My pulse quickens as the pages slow to a stop, and ink magically appears on it.

This is it.

This is my answer.

Of course, once I read the answer, part of me wishes I could go back to not knowing.

"What does it say?" Jax asks after a beat of silence goes by.

I swallow hard, my throat feeling very dry. "It says I used to be a guardian, but that changed. Now I'm..." I can barely breathe as I silently finish reading the rest of what the book is showing me.

Once I'm done, I slam the book shut, wanting to throw it out the damn window.

"What is it?" he asks with concern. When I make no effort to answer, he stops the car. Then he unbuckles his seatbelt, cups my cheeks, and forces me to look at him. "Tell me. I need to know."

I shake my head, fighting back the urge to scream. "It says I'm... That I'm a little bit of all the creatures that are linked to death. That I am death. That I'm not quite a creature because I'm not just a creature. I multiple ones... That I was created to become a weapon."

I can't believe this.

This isn't real.

This can't be happening.

Jax visibly pales. "Did it say who created you or why?"

I shake my head. "No, but..." I can't get the words to pass across my lips, but I can tell by Jax's expression that he's thinking the same thing as me.

That creating creatures are a specialty of one particular group.

"Jax, do you think that somehow the... Electi created me?" I finally push the words from my lips.

I want nothing more than for him to say no.

To lie to me.

But the healing wounds on our palms remind me that he can't.

"Maybe," he answers quietly.

It feels like every ounce of oxygen is ripped from my lungs. "But how?" I choke out. "Wouldn't I be able to remember something like that happening?"

He gives a very reluctant pause. "Memories can be tampered with."

"I know, but..." I growl in frustration and toss the book onto the backseat. "My parents would've told me if something like that happened to me." *I know they would have.*

He grows hesitant again. "Maybe they didn't know about it. I mean, I didn't know Pinkie possessed me until after it happened. And even now, I can't remember any of it."

True, but still... "The book could be lying." I'm starting to panic. "Maybe the pixie princess did something to it. I mean, she said it was a copy of the Scrawl of Secrets, so maybe it doesn't work right."

Pity fills in his eyes. "Maybe." But I can tell he doesn't think I'm right.

And honestly, deep down, I don't think I am either. From what I've experienced from my powers, from what I've seen in visions, everything connected to this new me is centered around death.

"But death really isn't a creature," I point out. "So *if* the book is right, what does that make me exactly? Or am I just nothing."

Jax shakes his head. "Alana, you're still you."

"No, I'm not. This... I can't."

"Hey." He cups my face again. "I know you're freaking out, but everything's going to be okay. Will figure this out."

"And how are we gonna do that?" I question. "That book was supposed to be our answer."

"Well, it kind of was," he says. "Or at least it's the starting point that leads to an answer."

"Yeah, I guess so," I mutter.

He offers me a sympathetic look before tucking a strand of my hair behind my ear. I should chew his butt out for the move, but my mind is racing so swiftly I can barely process anything.

This can't be happening. I'm Alana Avery, a guardian and that's it. I wasn't some experiment for the Electi. If I were, I'd know. If I were, I wouldn't be walking around in the world. I'd be their prisoner.

"So where is it leading us to now?" I ask as Jax drives forward and pulls out onto the highway.

"I think we should talk to your parents." He casts me a sidelong glance. "And see what they know. But I don't think it's safe to talk over the phone."

He's right. My phone has been bugged before. By Vivianne.

I nod, sinking into silence, fearing the end of the path we're headed down. Fearing my future. Fearing myself.

"Are you afraid of me?" I abruptly sputter. "I mean, the book says I was created by creatures linked to death."

Jax turns his head toward me, and I hold my breath as I wait for the truth to come out, knowing he has to be honest with me.

"No, I'm not," he says, and my heart rate settles the slightest bit. "I know we don't know much about what's going on, but I do know that you're not dangerous. I've seen way too much goodness in you."

I smile, but it's a bit forced. While I can be a good person sometimes, I've also seen myself do some terrible things. Like in the vision of the future where I painted the world in blood.

Painted it in death.

But I keep all those thoughts to myself for now and try to focus on doing something simple, focus on taking my next breath.

And that's the best thing you can do for right now. My grandpa's voice suddenly fills my head.

I straighten in the seat. "Grandpa?" I don't mean to say it aloud. The words just sort of slip out.

Jax's gaze snaps in my direction. "What?"

"I can hear him in my head again," I tell Jax then wait to hear from my grandpa again.

"I don't have much time before I fade again," he says. *"So I need to make this quick. Death is coming, Alana. I've seen it with my own eyes. It'll start with you, and it'll end with you. But you can control the outcome. You can control death. It's why you can still talk to me, why you can see the death of others. Your abilities may seem like a curse, but they don't have to be."*

"How?" I beg for an answer.

"The dagger. The answer is in the dagger. The dagger is what will either destroy you or save you. You just need to be ready." His voice starts to fade. *"I'm so sorry for what you're about to learn."*

"No, don't go yet," I beg, tears burning in my eyes. "Please."

But only silence fills my head.

"What did he say?" Jax asks as he shifts gears.

I blink the tears back, my heart aching in my chest. "He said the answers are in the dagger."

"The Dagger of Conspectu?" he asks and I nod. "You know where that is, right?"

"Yeah."

"Okay, where is it?"

"Just keep heading to my parent's place."

"Okay." He speeds up, flying down the road, and silence stretches between us again.

My mind begins to flood with questions. Questions that I fear the answers to. I mean, I knew I was a rare creature, but this... Maybe being created by the Electi...

I don't know if I can handle this.

"Everything's going to be okay," Jax abruptly says.

I glance at him. "You can honestly say that after everything we've learned?"

He nods then reaches over and squeezes my hand. Normally, I'd yank my hand away and give him a big lecture on touching me, especially while he's bonded to me, but considering what happened.... How alone I feel right now...

I hold onto his hand for dear life, crossing my fingers that what waits for me at the end of all of this isn't death.

That I'm not death.

That something good will come out of this.

Right as I think it, my phone pings with an incoming message.

When I read the message, I perk up a bit.

Jayse: I found the sprite that bit you. Meet me at the Steel Iron Veil.

"Jayse got the sprite that can cure me," I announce, breathing in relief.

Finally, a bit of good news.

"Really?" Jax appears a bit surprised.

I nod. "Yeah. He said to meet him at The Steel Iron Veil. Do you know where that is?"

He frowns. "Yeah. It's in vampire territory."

"Really?" I reread the message. "Why would he ask me to meet him there?"

"Maybe it's a trap," he mumbles, cracking his window and letting in the cool night breeze.

I shake my head. "Jayse wouldn't set me up."

He gives me a pressing look. "He might not, but the vampire in him might."

I glare at him. "No, Jayse would never do that to me."

But after everything that's happened, a bit of doubt weighs in my mind.

"I'm gonna text him back and see if I can get some more info," I tell Jax.

"Just be careful about what you say," Jax stresses. "Don't give out our location."

I give him a salute and send Jayse a reply, latching onto the distraction.

Me: Why do you want me to meet you there? Isn't that in vampire territory?

It takes him a moment to reply.

Jayse: Yeah... Look, Alana. Something's happened...

The message ends there.

So weird.

Me: What's going on?

Me: Jayse?

Me: Why won't you answer me?

After a couple of minutes tick by, I give up, fear pulsating through me.

"We need to go there," I inform Jax, putting my phone away. "I think Jayse is in trouble."

Jax shakes his head. "It's way too dangerous for you to be in vampire territory right now."

"I don't care about that." I cross my arms. "Jayse is my best friend, and if he needs my help, I'm going."

Deep down, I know it'll take more than a little speech to persuade Jax to do this. Well, at least with the old Jax it would. But the new one seems to listen to me more.

"We'll go there," he finally says with heavy reluctance, making me wonder if this bond he has with me is forcing him to obey me. "But we need to be careful about it, okay? And we need to have a plan."

I nod, in total agreement with Jax. I just hope I'm wrong. That Jayse is okay. But a strange sensation is forming in the pit of my stomach, a sense of death stirring inside me... It has me worried.

But I swallow hard, telling the sensation to shut the hell up. That death isn't going to appear now. And for the moment, the feeling goes quiet. But who the hell knows how long that'll last.

Who the hell knows how long I can keep death quiet.

ABOUT THE AUTHOR

Jessica Sorensen is a *New York Times* and *USA Today* best-selling author who lives in the snowy mountains of Wyoming. When she's not writing, she spends her time reading and hanging out with her family.

ALSO BY JESSICA SORENSEN

Guardian Academy Series:

Entranced

Entangled

Enchanted

The Forest of Shadow & Bones

Entice

Charmed

Untitled (coming soon)

Sunnyvale Series:

The Year I Became Isabella Anders

The Year of Falling in Love

The Year of Second Chances

The Year of Kai and Isa

Untitled (coming soon)

Enchanted Chaos Series:

Enchanted Chaos

Shimmering Chaos

Iridescent Chaos

Untitled (coming soon)

Monster Academy for the Magical:

Monster Academy for the Magical

Untitled (coming soon)

Capturing Magic:

Chasing Wishes

Chasing Magic

Untitled (coming soon)

Chasing the Harlyton Sisters Series:

Chasing Hadley

Falling for Hadley

Holding onto Hadley

Untitled (coming soon)

Cursed Hadley:

Cursed Hadley

Enchanting Hadley (coming soon)

Tangled Realms:

Forever Violet: Everlasting Moonlight

Forever Stardust: Everlasting Stardust

Untitled (coming soon)

Curse of the Vampire Queen:

Tempting Raven

Enchanting Raven

Alluring Raven

Untitled (coming soon)

<u>Unraveling You Series:</u>

Unraveling You

Raveling You

Awakening You

Inspiring You

Fated by Darkness

Untitled (coming soon)

<u>Unexpected Series:</u>

The Unexpected Complications of Revenge

Untitled (coming soon)

<u>Shadow Cove Series:</u>

What Lies in the Darkness

What Lies in the Dark

Untitled (coming soon)

<u>Mystic Willow Bay Series:</u>

The Secret Life of a Witch

Broken Magic

Stolen Kisses

One Wild, Crazy Zombie Night

Magical Whispers & the Undead

Untitled (coming soon)

<u>Standalones:</u>

The Forgotten Girl

<u>Honeyton Annabella:</u>

The Illusion of Annabella

Untitled (coming soon)

<u>Rebels & Misfits:</u>

Confessions of a Kleptomaniac

Rules of a Rebel and a Shy Girl

<u>The Heartbreaker Society:</u>

The Opposite of Ordinary

The Heartbreaker Society Curse

The Heartbreaker Society Secret (coming soon)

<u>Broken City Series:</u>

Nameless

Forsaken

Oblivion

Forbidden (coming soon)

<u>The Coincidence Series:</u>

The Coincidence of Callie and Kayden

The Redemption of Callie and Kayden

The Destiny of Violet and Luke

The Probability of Violet and Luke

The Certainty of Violet and Luke

The Resolution of Callie and Kayden

Seth & Greyson

The Evermore of Callie & Kayden

Untitled (coming soon)

The Secret Series:

The Prelude of Ella and Micha

The Secret of Ella and Micha

The Forever of Ella and Micha

The Temptation of Lila and Ethan

The Ever After of Ella and Micha

Lila and Ethan: Forever and Always

Ella and Micha: Infinitely and Always

Untitled (coming soon)

The Shattered Promises Series:

Shattered Promises

Fractured Souls

Unbroken

Broken Visions

Scattered Ashes

Untitled (coming soon)

Breaking Nova Series:

Breaking Nova

Saving Quinton

Delilah: The Making of Red

Nova and Quinton: No Regrets

Tristan: Finding Hope

Wreck Me

Ruin Me

Untitled (coming soon)

The Fallen Star Series:

The Fallen Star

The Underworld

The Vision

The Promise

The Lost Soul

The Evanescence

Untitled (coming soon)

The Darkness Falls Series:

Darkness Falls

Darkness Breaks

Darkness Fades

Untitled (coming soon)

The Death Collectors Series (NA and YA):

Ember X and Ember

Cinder X and Cinder

Spark X and Spark

Untitled (coming soon)

<u>**Unbeautiful Series:**</u>

Unbeautiful

Untamed

Untitled (coming soon)